CARL MAKES A SCRAPBOOK

Dear Sarah,
I give you this
scrapbook so that
you may keep a
history of those things
that you most love
and best remember.
love,
Aunt Shirley

·CARL MAKES A·
Scrapbook

Alexandra Day

Farrar, Straus and Giroux

New York

Also by Alexandra Day

Carl Goes Shopping
Carl's Christmas
Carl's Afternoon in the Park
Carl's Masquerade
Carl Goes to Daycare

To my mother,
who stocked the cupboards and helped us do it ourselves

My thanks to Emma Lord and her family,
and to A/C Ch. Wisteria's Bismark v Fruhling, A/C CDX

Copyright © 1994 by Alexandra Day
All rights reserved
Library of Congress catalog card number: 94–71633
Published simultaneously in Canada by HarperCollinsCanadaLtd
Color separations by Photolitho AG
Printed and bound in the United States of America by Berryville Graphics
First edition, 1994

I appreciate the time and effort which went into the many interesting entries in our Carl's Scrapbook Contest. We doubled the number of winners, but still wish that many more could have been included.

The winners are: VACATIONS: *Heidi Holmlund, for the snowy puppy.* HEROES & HEROINES: *Nancy Freeman, for the account of Kohl's heroics; Steve Powell, for the search-and-rescue dog Bronté; Jeff Huss, for the collector's card of Fox; Deni Lewis, for the story and picture about Jingles, the Dream Dog.* HOLIDAYS: *Tonja Deviney, for the witches; Judith Adams, for the chows at Christmas.* PICTURES & WORDS: *Marcia Snyder, for Penny smiling; Judy Hodnett, for the fawn and puppy; Joseph Bronstein, for "Better Than a Bone"; Marissa Mokaren (seven years old), for "Lucy"; Ermonie Young, for the dog and duck.*

The Carl character originally appeared in *Good Dog, Carl* by
Alexandra Day, published by Green Tiger Press

"While I'm out gardening, you two can watch this video about the alphabet."

myself at nine weeks

Madeleine at fifteen months

My aunt Hyacinth and her new baby

Chip and Edna

My brother Edward and me

Father and mother

The dogs of my childhood

The Aunts

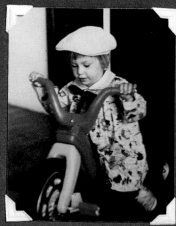

My Grandfather

My grandmother

Stephen and his College chums

Me at three

·MILESTONES·

From my bridal shower

Stephen on his first high school trip

My mother and I with my Lamaze instructor

The card from Aunt Shirley

Our honeymoon

Stephen's first client

Carl's first day with us

Stephen's first visit to Detroit

Carl and Madeleine ready to visit daycare

Our first home

· FRIENDS ·

Arlene, our personal
Auntie Mame

Thad - the seeker

Jeff
has a
highly
personal
style!

"Uncle" Edsel, who inspires
us all

Ellen and me at College

Harold, who grew up to have
enough energy for all of us

Anne, whom I met in
high school

Harmonia, whom we got to
know through Madeleine

Björn, an exchange
student and friend

Stephen's baseball
companion, Saul

I boarded with the Millers at College

Our Southern California journey

Beautiful Balboa Park in San Diego

Puppy Carl on our Northwest trip

Jai-alai

A Georgian Bay evening

Family and friends at Georgian Bay

Sea Stones Cottages . . Waldport, Oregon

On the beach in Oregon

Our second-anniversary trip

WATER FLOWER

·HEROES & HEROINES·

Mark Twain

Beatrix Potter

Audrey Hepburn

Ace of Hearts, the first dog in San Diego County to work as a registered therapy dog in the critical care unit of a hospital

Edith Wharton

Beethoven

Isak Dinesen

Mme Curie

BLACK BOB

THE DANDY WONDER DOG

BRIZO

JEFF HUSS & 'FOX'
POLICE CANINE TEAM
1992

Kohl–Four Times a Hero

This dog sensed trouble and rescued those who needed help. He saved his mistress in a medical emergency by rousing passers-by. Another time he urged her to the door of a neighbor, thought to be away on a trip. She entered and found the man bound and gagged by burglars. Again, when a woman and children were being threatened by an abusive husband, Kohl knocked the man down, suffering two knife slashes, and held him until police arrived. Finally, Kohl dragged a child from the arms of an abductor while her mother watched, frozen with horror.

Dream Dog

"I'm listening," thought Jingles, as Jonah's hand gently fingered the little dog's ear. The silver bell inside tinkled softly. With a contented sigh, baby was off to dreamland.

Nighttime was Jingles' busy time, as he chased down happy dreams to give to his child. He'd done it for over forty years, with Jonah's mother, and first with her older brother. Over the years he learned just where the glorious, "hope it never ends" dreams were kept.

Jonah smiled in his sleep as Jingles snuggled closer, eyes bright and shining, as his little bell tinkled in the night.

·HOLIDAYS·

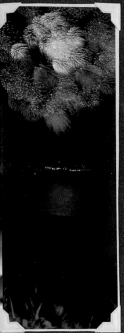

An old-fashioned card from Great-aunt Shirley

Our first family Christmas in our new house

Fireworks on the Bay, 1989

Stephen to me and me to Stephen, 1983

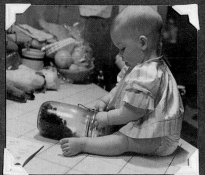

Madeline helping with Thanksgiving dinner

Patrick on his day

My brother Chip at nine

Another card from Aunt Shirley

"I'll Bee your Valentine"

6 PIECES No. 14

Grizzly BRAND

SUPREME QUALITY
SPARKLERS
MADE IN JAPAN

No. 14 GOLD COLORED
SPARKLERS

CAUTION
FLAMMABLE
SEE SIDE PANEL FOR
OTHER CAUTIONS

Whoof! Whoof!
Eyes Wishing You
A Merry Christmas.

My true Valentine

TO MY Valentine

I'm dog-gone glad that someone,
Has promised to be mine.
I'm dog-gone glad that someone,
Is you my Valentine.

John Singer Sargent

This reminds me of Grandma's
house on the lake

Babies are the same
in all ages

An Old chocolate ad

Sent to me by Anne

My mother brought me this from Boston

Better Than A Bone

Outside this fence,
I'm sure there may be...
Wild friends and buried bones,
Just waiting for me,
They will have to wait,
Because my place is here,
Where I'm loved and cuddled...
Where I want to be.

—Joseph Bronstein

Lucy

Lucy is a bad dog. Lucy digs holes. Lucy walks through the garden. Lucy begs at the table. Lucy barks at the sky. She chased the mailman. Lucy is five years older than me so she should know better. I am seven so she is twelve, which is really old in dog years. I feel sorry for her when she gets in trouble. She looks like she is sorry. She says "please" with her face. We all still love Lucy. But tomorrow that old dog will dig another hole. I think she enjoys it.

— by Marissa (age 7)

"You've both been very good.
Did you learn a lot?"